MR. MEN
The Big Match

Roger Hargreaves

Original concept by
Roger Hargreaves

Written and illustrated by
Adam Hargreaves

EGMONT

Mr Small was very excited.

It was the big football match on Saturday and Mr Small loved football.

But there was a problem.

Mr Small was … a bit too small.

But Mr Small was determined to play. On Saturday he arrived at the football field all ready to go. He really hoped he'd be picked for the team.

The big match was Happyland against The Bossy Boots.

Mr Happy was the captain of Happyland and his team was all organised.

Little Miss Bossy was, of course, captain of
The Bossy Boots.

She began picking the team.

But some were not very suitable.

For instance, she did not pick Mr Strong because he
was much too strong. He burst the ball every time he
kicked it!

And she did not pick Little Miss Splendid because she was wearing quite the wrong sort of shoes and she refused to wear football boots!

And Mr Mischief … well, he kept moving the goal posts!

But, eventually, Little Miss Bossy did choose her team.

Finally there was only one place left and the choice was between Mr Jelly and Mr Small.

She picked Mr Jelly.

Poor Mr Small. He was very disappointed.

The two teams took their positions on the pitch and Mr Noisy, the referee, blew his whistle.

A terrifically loud whistle!

So loud that Mr Jelly took fright and ran away.

"Bother," said Little Miss Bossy. "OK! Small, you're on!"

Mr Small was delighted. He was going to get to play after all.

The big match started and it was soon easy to see that the Happyland team were far better than The Bossy Boots.

Especially because they had Mr Tickle in goal.

His long arms saved every shot.

And Mr Small quickly realised that he was not going to have much chance of showing off his skills. to have much chance of showing off his skills.

Nobody passed the ball to him.

Poor Mr Small.

Just before half time, Mr Happy scored the first goal for Happyland.

Mr Forgetful, who was The Bossy Boots' goalkeeper, had forgotten why he was there.

So at half time Little Miss Bossy put Little Miss Somersault in goal.

What a difference!

She was brilliant.

So brilliant she even scored a goal at the other end as well!

With only five minutes to play, the score was one all.

And Mr Small had not touched the ball even once.

And then a long ball kicked forward by Little Miss Helpful landed just in front of Mr Tickle.

He reached out one long arm, but as he tried to pick it up the ball suddenly moved to the left.

"That's odd," he thought.

He tried to pick it up again and the ball rolled to the right.

The ball zigzagged forwards, then it darted left and slid right.

Each time Mr Tickle reached for it, the ball was too quick.

Before Mr Tickle knew what was going on, the ball had rolled over the goal line!

And Mr Noisy blew the final whistle.

"I don't understand," said a very confused Mr Tickle.

And then Mr Small stepped out from behind the ball.

Mr Small had scored the winning goal!

He was awarded man of the match.

Small man of the big match!